The L___ ___l

written by Pam Holden
illustrated by Lamia Aziz

"Look at my little tail,"
said Rabbit.
"My tail is a very good tail."

"Who has a long tail like that?" said Rabbit.

"That's my tail," said Snake.
"It's good for sliding.
You can't slide with your tail."

4

"Who has a fat tail like
that?" said Rabbit.

"That's my tail," said Kangaroo.
"It's good for jumping.
You can't jump with your tail."

"Who has a little tail like that?" said Rabbit.

"That's my tail," said Fish.
"It's good for swimming.
You can't swim with your tail."

"Who has a fat tail like
that?" said Rabbit.

"That's my tail," said Crocodile.
"It's good for hitting.
You can't hit with your tail."

"Who has a long tail like that?" said Rabbit.

"That's my tail," said Bird.
"It's good for flying.
You can't fly with your tail."

"Who has a long tail like that?" said Rabbit.

"That's my tail," said Monkey.
"It's good for swinging.
You can't swing with your tail."

"Who has a fat tail like that?" said Rabbit.

"That's not my tail.
It's my trunk," said Elephant.
"Here is my tail.
It's a good tail for holding."